ACCLAIM FOR STORIES BY
CURTIS SITTENFELD

You Think It, I'll Say It

'There is no writer alive who inhabits her characters
so knowingly, or is able to send up contemporary
attitudes and mores as expertly . . . clever, funny,
revealing and a joy to read'
EVENING STANDARD

'Fans won't be disappointed: the tales here condense
lifetimes of confusion, betrayal and bad decisions into
perfect miniatures of American prose'
GUARDIAN

'Clear-eyed and compulsive'
MAIL ON SUNDAY

'Funny, smart, pin-sharp'
GOOD HOUSEKEEPING

WITHDRAWN
FROM
STOCK

Help Yourself

Help Yourself

Stories

Curtis Sittenfeld

doubleday

TRANSWORLD PUBLISHERS
Penguin Random House, One Embassy Gardens,
8 Viaduct Gardens, London SW11 7BW
www.penguin.co.uk

Transworld is part of the Penguin Random House group of companies
whose addresses can be found at global.penguinrandomhouse.com

Penguin
Random House
UK

First published in Great Britain in 2020 by Doubleday
an imprint of Transworld Publishers

The stories in this collection have been previously published as follows:
'White Women LOL' in *O, the Oprah Magazine*; 'Show Don't Tell' in
The New Yorker; 'Creative Differences' in *New York* magazine.

A CIP catalogue record for this book
is available from the British Library.

ISBN 9780857527479

Typeset in 11.5/15.5pt ITC Galliard Std by Jouve (UK), Milton Keynes
Printed and bound in Great Britain by Clays Ltd, Elcograf S.p.A.

Penguin Random House is committed to a sustainable
future for our business, our readers and our planet. This book
is made from Forest Stewardship Council® certified paper.

For
Jennifer Rudolph Walsh
&
Marianne Velmans,
with great affection

Contents

White Women LOL

Kiwi the Shih Tzu gets loose on the Thursday before the schools in the district let out for winter break. This means everyone knows, in a way they might not if he got loose after break had started. Regardless, everyone knows Kiwi. He weighs maybe twelve pounds, and the plentiful white fur around his face accentuates his dark eyes and dark little nose. (Do dogs have faces? Jill isn't sure). But Kiwi is both yippy and cute, and, though Jill – who is not particularly a dog lover – has never sought to pet him, he's the only dog at the elementary school drop-off whose name she knows.

Aside from his cuteness, there are probably two other reasons Kiwi is a school celebrity: the first is that he belongs to the Johnson family, and Vanessa Johnson herself is something of a celebrity. She's an anchor on Channel 8 evening news, is widely agreed to be the most beautiful mother at

Hardale East Elementary School, is black, and lives in the tree-lined, large-house-filled neighborhood adjacent to the school, which allows her to bring Kiwi on a leash when she walks with her children to school in the morning; meanwhile, almost all of the school's other black families, whose children account for under ten per cent of the student body, live miles to the north, and ride the bus to campus. The second reason for Kiwi's celebrity is that, for kids, including Jill's own son and daughter, Shih Tzu is fun to say.

The way Kiwi escapes is that the Johnsons' housecleaner, who has been working for them on a weekly basis for years, carries a bag of garbage outside to the trash bin, leaves the back door open, and doesn't securely close the storm door. Apparently, while the housecleaner is despondent, Vanessa Johnson doesn't blame her; Kiwi is wily, and such a thing could have happened on anyone's watch. But, as Jill hears from her best friend Amy, whose other best friend is Vanessa, it isn't the first time the housecleaner has let this happen. However, in the other instances, Kiwi didn't make it out of the backyard.

It's from Amy that Jill learns about Kiwi. At 9 p.m. Thursday, Amy texts her, *Kiwi has been missing since noon!*

This is the first text Amy has sent Jill in weeks, and Jill immediately replies, *Oh no what happened?*

Amy explains the situation, and Jill expresses concern, which she does feel, though perhaps not as much as an actual dog lover would and not a concern totally separate from her own concerns about her strained friendship with Amy and her – Jill's – recently tarnished standing in the community. Jill initially thinks she's learning about a dog's imminent death rather than its escape; she thinks she's feeling a conclusive sorrow rather than the agitated hope of the unresolved. Their neighborhood is a grid of quiet, stately residential avenues bound by significantly busier streets. Additionally, in their part of the Midwest, a cold front is expected for the weekend and the temperature will likely fall to the single digits.

Jill and Amy engage in a thirteen-text volley, and the last text between them, from Jill, is *Wow I feel so bad, keep me posted*

She refrains from adding:

Does everyone at school hate me?

Is it too soon for me to come back to drop-off?

Are we still friends?

Almost three weeks prior, Amy's husband Rick hosted her fortieth-birthday party in the elegantly appointed back room of a trendy downtown restaurant. There was a fireplace, a bar, and many high round tables where guests could congregate first for drinks and then for the buffet dinner. Instead of flowers, there were willow branches and white lights.

About four dozen people were in attendance, the majority of them Hardale East Elementary School parents. Jill drank two glasses of wine and participated in several enjoyable conversations: one with Joanna Thomas and Wendy Upson about whether Mrs Pogue, who was all of their daughters' first-grade teacher, was pregnant; one with Sarah

O'Dell about what per cent reprehensible Ivanka Trump was (Jill said 99 per cent, Sarah said 200 per cent); and one with Stewart Nowacki about the candy-cane-patterned pants he was wearing. Stewart Nowacki was Jill's go-to for harmless married flirtation, and when she'd learned that he was also her friend Rose's go-to for harmless married flirtation, it had enhanced rather than diminished her own flirtation with him because then she and Rose could jokily compare notes as well as speculate about whether Stewart and his wife Megan still had sex. Jill didn't speak to Vanessa Johnson, though she did end up at the bar at the same time as Vanessa's husband Bobby; as was often the case at such gatherings, Vanessa and Bobby were the only black people present. Jill and Bobby warmly exclaimed about how hard it was to believe that the busy month of December had arrived already.

The birthday cake was exceptional: hazelnut-almond topped with dark-chocolate ganache and white-chocolate truffles. The party was just winding down, with a third or so of the guests having departed, when Jill emerged from the restroom and noticed a table of five people who hadn't been there when she'd entered the restroom. They were black.

They were black, and they were stylish: two women and three men, all probably a little younger than Amy and Jill. One woman wore a floral silk blouse with a maroon background, and the other a black shrug over a beige camisole. Of the men, one wore a coat and tie, one a coat without a tie, and the third an orange cravat.

They weren't Amy's friends – they weren't guests – because

Jill would have known them if they were. It was impossible that Amy would have friends close enough for inclusion at her birthday party whom Jill had never met. Jill also knew they weren't Amy's guests because they weren't mingling. And did she know because they were black? Sure, of course – also that.

She approached their table. In the time since, she has vacillated between attempting to re-create her own mindset and to permanently erase it from her memory. She thinks she was trying harder than usual – harder than she would have with a group of white people – to seem friendly and diplomatic. Though her first words to the group were not recorded, what she had said was 'I realize this might not be obvious, but there's a private party going on in this room. A birthday party.'

The two women and three men looked at her with varying degrees of amusement and irritation. Jill added, 'You're not friends of Vanessa and Bobby, are you?'

After a pause, the woman in the floral blouse said, 'No. We're not friends of Vanessa and Bobby.'

'If you wouldn't mind taking your drinks to the main room,' Jill said, and, though she was unaware of it in the moment, the recording had started, 'I think that would be best.'

With undisguised contempt, the man wearing the cravat said, 'Oh, really? Is that what you think?'

'I'm not trying to be—' For the first time, Jill faltered. 'It's my friend Amy's birthday, and her husband rented this room. That's all.'

The woman in the blouse said, also contemptuously, 'Do you feel unsafe? Are you going to call the cops?'

'Am I going to call the cops?' Jill was repeating these words, she is certain, in bewilderment at the escalation. But she concedes that, in the video, if one is inclined toward such an interpretation, her tone might come off as more contemplative. 'This isn't—' she began, but expressing herself had, abruptly, become very challenging. She said, 'This isn't political. I just think you'd all be more comfortable in the other room.'

'Bless your heart,' the man in the cravat said. 'Bless your heart for not making this *political*.'

One of the other two men, the one not wearing a tie, said, 'Your friend's party is over. The room was rented until ten o'clock.' He held out his left arm, and on his wrist was a steel and white-gold watch, which was, as it happened, the same watch worn by Jill's husband Ken. The time displayed was 10:20.

In a mocking voice, the woman in the blouse said, 'Sorry!' And, with fake cheer, the man in the cravat said, 'So that's why they're letting in the Negro riffraff!'

'That's not at all what I meant,' Jill said.

One of the men hadn't spoken, and one of the women hadn't, either; the woman was the one using her phone to record the encounter, as Jill subsequently deduced from the angle of the camera. The man with the watch said, 'Just like you, we're trying to enjoy an evening out. Could you leave us alone?' His voice contained no note of sarcasm, and later Jill wished she had taken her cue from him.

Instead, she folded her arms and sighed, and even she must admit that, in the video, the sigh is peevish, not compassionate or repentant. But the man in the cravat and the woman in the blouse were being so rude! Over a sincere misunderstanding! Jill said, 'Well, I didn't realize what time it was.'

The woman in the blouse laughed mirthlessly. This is where the recording ends.

By late Friday afternoon – the last day of school before winter break, more than twenty-four hours after Kiwi's escape – fliers blanket the neighborhood. There is one on the lamp post outside Jill's family's house, which Jill spies from her living-room window and, though she's still mostly hiding indoors almost three weeks after Amy's birthday party, she walks out to examine it.

In big letters at the top, the flier says *LOST DOG*, then there's a phone number, then there's a large color photo of Kiwi looking particularly adorable, his tongue hanging out, then in smaller print it says: *Our beloved Kiwi has been missing since 12/21. Please call if you see him!! He loves dog treats, especially Doggy Did brand turkey liver flavor and might approach if you shake a container of them. Call any time day or night!!!*

Already, Jill has received a mass email from Vanessa containing all the same information, with the additional hopeful tidbit (this is how Jill realizes that they are not exactly on a canine death watch) that Kiwi was spotted early this morning in a yard on Goodridge Lane, though he ran away when the person tried to read his tags, and the additional factual tidbit that live traps are being set up at three locations. The email, which was forwarded to Jill four other times after she received it from Vanessa (Jill takes it as a positive sign that she still makes her acquaintances' forwarding cut), ended with an appeal to repost or at least reply to Vanessa's posts about Kiwi on Facebook and Nextdoor so as to make them appear more prominently in people's feeds.

As Jill re-enters her house, she can hear the competing sounds of her children's iPads in the kitchen; her daughter, who is six, is watching YouTube videos of a tween singer, and her son, who is ten, is watching YouTube videos of other kids playing video games. She would repost Vanessa's Facebook posts, Jill thinks, if she were still on Facebook. But almost three weeks ago, she deleted her account.

It was the man with the cravat – it turned out his name was Ronald William Fitzsimmons IV, and he was a curator at the contemporary art museum – who posted the video on Facebook the day after Amy's party. His comment read, *Committed the crime of drinking $16 cocktails while black last night . . . white women LOL.*

By the time Jill learned of the post, the video had been up for two hours, been viewed 937 times, and shared 201. The responses included:

 – *Ronald so sorry you had to endure this, that woman is idiotic garbage*
 – *White privilege is a hell of a drug*
 – *Internet, do your thing, let's find out who Vodka Vicky is*

There was a long comment that started, *As a white woman who has been doing a lot of soul-searching lately . . .* and the rest was so tedious that, even under the circumstances, Jill skimmed it. There was a GIF of a fair-haired white man blinking (posted by a black man) and another GIF of a cartoon rat shaking his finger in disapproval (posted by a black woman) and another GIF of a baby spitting out what looked like pureed peas in abject disgust (posted by a white woman).

In response to the exhortation to find out who the woman was, there was a comment from Joanna Thomas, one of the people with whom Jill had speculated about whether their daughters' teacher was pregnant. *I was at this party and I know this woman,* Joanna had written. *She is not a bad person and it's sad to me we live in such divisive times.*

Under Joanna's comment, another mother from Hardale East Elementary School, a woman Jill knew in passing, had written, *Your silence will not protect you, Joanna. Obviously, that's Jill Gershin.*

The woman had tagged Jill, which was how she found Ronald William Fitzsimmons IV's original post and also, presumably, how strangers began to denounce her directly by tagging her when they shared the video. The first message began, *Lady you should of minded your own damn business . . .* The second, which was where she stopped, said in its entirety, *Ha ha Vodka Vicky, did you buy that dress at Talbots?*

On Saturday morning, Jill's alarm goes off at six-thirty, an hour later than she sets it during the week; ever since the incident, she's preferred to get her workouts in while her neighbors are sleeping. It's still mostly dark, and a not terrible thirty-eight degrees, when she leaves the house, running west on Vista Boulevard. In her earbuds, she listens to an economics podcast; prior to the incident, she usually streamed pop mixes, but is she still allowed to listen to Rihanna and Beyoncé?

Jill has been jogging for twenty minutes, and the sky is more light than dark, when, shockingly, she sees Kiwi. Kiwi! Out of nowhere! So small and white-furred, and so surprisingly fast. He's fifteen feet away? By this point, Jill is on Tyler Drive, which is a half-mile loop off Vista Boulevard. Kiwi is scampering across the sprawling front yard of a sprawling brick colonial house. Within seconds, he's forty feet away. Jill is filled with adrenaline. What should her strategy be?

'Kiwi!' she cries, just as the dog disappears around the side of the house. Jill darts over the frost-covered grass, tracking Kiwi's path onto the driveway, under a porte cochere supported by Ionic columns, and into the backyard, which features a brick terrace and no sign of Kiwi. This is crushing. Jill doesn't know who lives here. Should she knock on their door? It's just after seven. If only she'd procured a container of turkey-liver treats!

She turns in a circle, scanning the backyard, just in case. The grass beyond the terrace abuts a wooded area of a dozen or so acres – Tyler Drive is the fanciest street in the neighborhood, with a stone arch marking its only entrance – and Jill assumes Kiwi is somewhere in there.

She pulls her phone from the thigh pocket of her leggings and, with trembling fingers, texts Amy, *Just saw Kiwi!!! On Tyler drive. What's Vanessa number? Couldn't catch him ynfortunateky*

Amy takes seven minutes to respond. By then, Jill has started to feel weird about her presence in a stranger's backyard, so she returns to the street, and, still confused about a course of action, continues jogging.

Amy's first text is a blue bubble containing Vanessa's contact information. Her second is *Great!!* Her third reads, *U know about change of plan? Kiwi runs away whenever people see him.* Her fourth text is a screenshot of a Facebook post from Vanessa. *Update on our precious pup: The animal rescue experts are telling us he's now 'in flight mode' so if you see him, it's VERY likely he will run away from you. You have 2 choices, 1 is do the opposite of what I said before (smh) – Don't chase him, don't call his name, don't do anything except call me or Bobby ASAP. Choice 2 is – Lie down on the ground acting like you're hurt, moan and whimper, get in fetal position, and he might come over to 'help' you. This doesn't sound crazy at all, right? Thank you friends <3*

Jill stops jogging to read the post twice. She texts back, *Yikes.* Then she texts Vanessa about the sighting – *It's Jill Gershin, I saw Kiwi less than 10 min ago at 27 Tyler Drive but he ran northwest* – and Vanessa texts back, *Oh wow many thanks Jill! Bobby and I are about to go looking so we will start there.* She includes the emoji that Jill thinks of as either praying hands or gratitude, though maybe it's both.

Amy does not reply.

A few years earlier, in order to be more present with her family, Jill had turned off her push notifications for Facebook. Thus, it had been her friend Rose – the one with whom Jill shared the harmless crush on Stewart Nowacki – who, semi-inadvertently, alerted Jill to the video. Around 3 p.m. that Sunday, the day after the birthday party, Rose texted, *Jill I think that thing on FB is so unfair to you. Hope you're hanging in there.* Immediately, uneasiness flared up in Jill, or maybe it was more that a bad feeling had been coursing through her body since the birthday party and it was then that it coalesced. Jill texted back *Um . . . what thing on FB?* But she checked without waiting for Rose's reply.

She watched the video and read the comments while perched on a small antique rocking chair in an alcove of the upstairs hallway, a piece of furniture it was possible that no member of her family had ever used; she'd received Rose's text on her way to the master bedroom to grab a basket of dirty laundry. Sitting on the rocker, Jill wondered if she might faint. This was horrifying. It was horrifying in several different ways. Did the video really show what it purported to show? Would she be fired from her job? (She was a senior project manager at the corporate headquarters of a chain of regional supermarkets). Were her children now in danger? Did her family need to move to a different state?

She texted Amy, *Can u call me?*

When Amy didn't call within forty seconds, Jill went to find Ken, who was in the kitchen boiling water for a priming solution for the beer he brewed at home. Ken did not have a Facebook account or otherwise participate in social media, and tended, as a point of pride, to feign incomprehension about its vernacular. In this instance, however, perhaps due to Jill's agitation, he did not showily request a definition of terms. 'This is the kind of thing that could end up on *Good Morning America*, Jill said.

As they watched the video together, she again felt that she might faint. On second viewing, she knew she didn't come off well. But surely she didn't come off as officially racist, like those white people in Target or at delis yelling at immigrants for wearing turbans or speaking Spanish. Did she?

She said to Ken, 'How bad do you think it is?'

Mildly, he said, 'If you thought they were crashing Amy's party, it would have been better to ask the restaurant manager to talk to them.'

'Yes, obviously,' Jill snapped. 'Should I time-travel back to last night and do that instead?'

Ken shrugged. 'Don't viral videos blow over in a day or two?'

'I'm not sure,' she said. 'This is my first time starring in one.' When Ken didn't respond, she added, 'Are you worried about our family's safety?'

Still mildly, he said, 'In what sense?'

'Forget it.' She went back upstairs, texting Amy as she

climbed the steps. *Are u around? Really need to talk. Kind of freaking out.*

When Amy still hadn't responded within half an hour, Jill texted, *Where are u? Is everything ok?* An hour later, she texted, *Seriously I'm getting worried.*

Amy called her just after 9 p.m., following a five-hour stretch in which Jill had not left the house. Instead of accompanying Ken and their daughter to their son's basketball game, Jill had stayed in, and rather than meeting her family for dinner afterward at the pizza place they often went to on Sundays, Jill had had the pizza delivered to their house. When Jill answered Amy's call, she said, 'Thank God. Where have you been all day?'

Amy sighed. 'Yeah, this really sucks.'

'So you've seen it?'

'Yes,' Amy said. 'I've seen it.'

'I mean, when people go looking for evidence of something, of course they'll find it.'

'Well, it's not like they had to look that hard.'

Jill was shocked. 'Wait,' she said. 'Do you think I'm some kind of white supremacist?'

'I think the whole thing is just awkward and embarrassing.' Jill assumed Amy meant embarrassing to Jill, until Amy added, 'I wish you hadn't mentioned that it was *my* birthday.'

For several hours, Jill had been imagining that, in her best-friend capacity, Amy would say something wise and comforting and, ideally, exculpatory. To encounter the opposite from Amy was far more upsetting than from Ken.

'It also might have been nice to have a heads-up that it happened,' Amy was saying.

'I had no idea they were recording it,' Jill said. 'I didn't know it would have an afterlife. Honestly, I thought I was doing you a favor. If one of the bathroom stalls had run out of toilet paper and I'd seen a roll nearby, I'd have replaced it myself instead of bothering you at your own party.'

'You might want to give some thought to that comparison,' Amy said. 'Black people and a roll of toilet paper – that's really problematic.'

Jill considered pointing out that, as problematicness went, until the previous year, Amy had referred to the black students who were bussed to Hardale East Elementary School as 'deseg kids', as in *desegregation*. Amy had attended Hardale East in the 1980s, and that was the term she'd grown up with; Jill, who had grown up in a different city, delicately said one day, 'I think these days we call them transfer students.'

On the phone, Jill said, 'Have you talked to Vanessa about the video?'

'Yes,' Amy said.

'And?'

'What do you want me to say? It's not a good look.'

'Was she extra offended?'

'Well, it's weird for her because she knows you.'

'You don't think she'll bring it up on the news, do you?'

'If you're stressing, call her.' Amy sighed again. 'I can't believe that all the people I didn't invite know about my party now.'

———

The Johnson family – Vanessa, Bobby, and their twin seven-year-old sons – were supposed to fly to Sarasota for Christmas with Bobby's extended family. They were supposed to leave Saturday morning, December twenty-third, but they delayed their departure; apparently, the boys are inconsolable. Bobby and the twins did fly out Sunday morning – Kiwi has now been missing for three days – and Vanessa has stayed behind in the hope of catching Kiwi in time for them all to be together on Christmas Day.

Jill learns this when she runs into her neighbor Eileen on Sunday afternoon at a pet-products megastore, where Jill has gone to buy Doggy Did brand turkey-liver treats and finds Eileen doing the same. Other dog treats are sold at her usual grocery store, Jill discovered, but not the Doggy Did turkey-liver kind. Jill isn't even sure that the recommendation to shake a treats container at Kiwi stands, but she dreamed last night that she caught Kiwi, and what if the dream was a premonition? When she awakened, it seemed imperative she do *something*. Also, the predicted temperature plunge has occurred, and now it's ten degrees outside.

Jill additionally learns from Eileen that a fox was caught yesterday in one of the three live traps set for Kiwi, then the fox was freed; and that, as enticement, the traps contain hot dogs and Vanessa Johnson's pajamas.

'How's Vanessa holding up?' Jill asks.

'I heard she hasn't slept since Thursday.'

'Is it because she doesn't have any pajamas to wear?' Jill says.

Does Eileen not laugh because she doesn't think it's funny or because of Jill's status as a pariah?

'Because she's so worried,' Eileen says.

'Right,' Jill says. 'Of course.'

She was not fired from her job. But when she returned to work after the incident, she was summoned to a meeting with her boss, the director of human resources, and the assistant general counsel, and told that she was being suspended with pay until January second, while an investigation determined whether she'd violated company policy by engaging in 'racial misconduct'. Although Jill wasn't sure she should be signing anything without a lawyer of her own, she did so, agreeing to the terms, which included no media contact – an unnecessary stipulation. The entire meeting was an out-of-body experience; the director of human resources was named Suzanne, and, for God's sake, when Suzanne had been pregnant, Jill had given her her own maternity clothes. Also, perhaps not coincidentally, Suzanne and Jill were Facebook friends.

During the two hours Jill was at work that day, three colleagues said something to her. A white man named Bruce said as they waited for an elevator, 'They sure have gotten entitled, haven't they?' Jill was horrified and changed the subject. A white woman named Peg said as Jill returned to her office, as if this were a compliment, 'Jill, you're famous!' Jill was horrified and fake-smiled. And another white woman named Helen stopped by Jill's office and said, 'My church has started hosting a monthly dialogue between the races. I met an African-American grandma named Mother Bernice at one of them, and she's not angry at all. She's not about assigning blame. She's all about love, and she's become like a family member to me. I want to invite you to the next dialogue.'

'I'll keep that in mind,' Jill said.

There were, in Jill's sixty-person division, two black employees, one named Sheila and one named Paul. She did not work closely with either of them, and neither of them said anything to her.

After the HR meeting, she managed to make it to her car before bursting into tears, and, after a few minutes, she pulled herself together enough to call Ken.

'Suspended *with* pay?' he said. 'Not without.'

'Yes,' Jill said. 'With.'

'Well, hey,' he said. 'You get an extra month of vacation.'

At home in her kitchen, Jill does not think Ken is paying attention as she unloads her bags from the grocery store and the pet-products store, but when she sets the clear cylinder of dog treats on the counter, he says in a wry tone, 'Wow.'

Jill says nothing.

'I hate to be the bearer of bad news,' he says, 'but you do know that even if you're the one who catches Kiwi, it doesn't offset what happened at Amy's birthday, right?'

Jill still says nothing.

'It's interesting how Kiwi has mobilized people,' Ken says. 'If our neighbors paid a fraction of the attention they're giving a dog to inequities in public education, what could be achieved?'

'You know what?' Jill says. 'Maybe if you joined Face-book, you could find a like-minded community who'd be interested in discussing this topic.'

In the end, the video seemed to have gone local-viral more than viral-viral. It did not end up on *Good Morning America,* or even on the local news – not on Channel 8 with Vanessa nor on the other stations – and strangers did not come to Jill's house to condemn her.

But at dinner, on that Monday after Ronald William Fitzsimmons IV posted the video, Jill's daughter, Becca, who was in first grade, said, 'Mommy, why don't you like people with brown skin?'

Jill and Becca were seated on one side of the kitchen table, and Ken and their son Josh, who was in fourth grade, were on the other. Jill made frantic eye contact with Ken. She swallowed her bite of the meatloaf she'd had abundant time to make that day after being sent home from the office and said, 'Of course I don't not like people with brown skin. People who are Jewish like us know that it's very important to speak out against all forms of prejudice.'

'Then why did you yell at them?' Becca said.

'I didn't,' Jill said. 'There was a misunderstanding.'

'Did a teacher say something to you, or did a student?' Ken asked Becca.

Josh said, 'Mom, why are they calling you Vodka Vicky when your name is Jill?'

That morning, instead of Jill walking with the children the two blocks to school drop-off, Ken had driven them, and in the weeks after, he continued to do so. Instead of lingering at drop-off, as was Jill's habit, he'd drive on to work without emerging from the car to chat with the other neighborhood parents – mostly mothers, some holding coffee or dog leashes, congregating outside for a few minutes before the ones with jobs went to work and the ones without jobs went to do Jill didn't really know what. This was how and where Jill had made Kiwi's acquaintance.

At the end of the day, Ken also was now the one to get the children from aftercare. Because of Jill's job suspension, aftercare was not currently necessary, but she decided it was best for the children to maintain their routine.

It's bitterly cold on Christmas morning. During her run, Jill turns from Vista Boulevard onto Tyler Drive and sees Vanessa squatting by an empty cage just behind the stone arch. This is the fourth day of Kiwi's absconsion.

So as not to startle Vanessa, Jill says her name when she's still several feet away. When Vanessa looks up, she says, 'Oh. Hi, Jill.' Vanessa stands.

It's only when she gets closer that Jill realizes she has never before seen Vanessa without makeup. She's seen her with TV makeup, when Vanessa attends school events directly after delivering the news, but Jill didn't realize until now that Vanessa wears subtler makeup at morning drop-off. On this morning, Vanessa still looks beautiful – she has almond-shaped eyes, smooth skin, and long, loosely curled hair over which she wears a red fleece hat – but she's palpably weary and anxious. Steam emerges from both their mouths.

Jill says, 'Did you decide not to go to Florida?'

'I'm headed to the airport after this,' Vanessa says. 'I come back tomorrow at noon.'

'I can check the traps while you're away. We don't celebrate Christmas so I'm not busy.'

'Dave Duncan organized a Google doc with different shifts. I think it's full, but if you tell him you're available for backup, that's great in case people forget. And Dave's the one to call if Kiwi *is* in the cage – he'll take Kiwi to his house. We're not supposed to get him out of the cage outside because if he gets loose again, we're really screwed.'

'Got it,' Jill says. Dave Duncan's son is on the same basketball team as Jill's son, and she considers Dave an asshole because of the way he yells from the sidelines at games. Does she need to revise this opinion?

'And I'll be back in twenty-four hours.' Abruptly, Vanessa looks like she's about to cry. In a breathless voice, she says, 'Jill, there's only one present I care about giving my kids this year.'

'I know,' Jill says. 'We all want it for them.' When she steps forward and hugs Vanessa, there are easily eight layers of parka, fleece and long underwear between them. Does Vanessa mind being hugged by the person in the video? Have the events of the last week buried the video? As a choked sob escapes from Vanessa, Jill thinks for the first time about why it is that they're not really friends. The most obvious reason is that Vanessa is intimidatingly beautiful; also, doesn't Vanessa's friendship with Amy establish some minor rivalry between Vanessa and Jill? But does the latter explanation hold, when Jill and Amy share other friends? They're still hugging when Jill says, 'Maybe in the new year, we could have a drink some time. And hopefully celebrate Kiwi's safe return.'

'I'd like that,' Vanessa says as they pull apart.

'The video from Amy's birthday,' Jill adds. 'I don't know if you purposely didn't mention it on TV or if it just wasn't newsworthy, but it's – that's not who I really am.'

Vanessa's expression changes. It changes from distraught and open to impatient and closed.

Jill says, 'I mean, not that having a drink would be racial at all. It would just be like neighbors—'

Vanessa holds up one gloved hand. 'Jill,' she says, and shakes her head. 'I don't have the bandwidth now.'

Two years ago, after an unarmed black seventeen-year-old boy in their city was fatally shot by a white police officer (not to be confused with the unarmed black men and boys fatally shot by white police officers in other cities), Jill marched downtown while carrying a sign that said, *If you want peace, work for justice.* Around that time, she made a donation to the NAACP. Well, she thought of making a donation to the NAACP. She can't remember if she actually did. But if she didn't, it was because it slipped her mind, not because she chose not to.

She knows the things white people aren't supposed to say: *Can I touch your hair?* and *I don't see race* or, even worse, *I don't care if a person is black or white or green or purple or polka-dotted.* She would *never* say those things.

She knows what a micro-aggression is. She knows what *woke* means. Even though she's forty-one and lives in the Midwest, she knows what it means!

But also: After her cousin Maureen's divorce from her terrible husband was finalized, Jill texted her, *Free at last, free at last, thank god almighty ur free at last.*

Also also: One weekend last summer, Jill drove her children forty minutes to a state park to swim in a river she'd always heard was nice, and when they got to the beach, there were three other families there, all black, and Jill said to her kids, 'Wait, don't get out of the car,' and her son said, 'Why?' and Jill said, 'Just hold on, there's something I need to check.' She group texted two friends: *Have u ever been to Redbird State Park? Would u let ur kids swim there?* As she waited for responses, she Googled *Redbird River clean*, then *Redbird River polluted*, then *Redbird safe to swim*. It wasn't that she didn't want her children swimming with the other families, and it wasn't that she was unacquainted with the fraught history of race and swimming. It was that could this be a Flint situation, where the water was dirty but no one in charge cared because it wasn't supposed to affect white people. Her Google searches turned up various touristy descriptors: *A beloved spot for fishing and canoeing, with gorgeous views.* Then Amy texted, *Never been but heard it's awesome* and Rose texted *Ted and I were there a LONG time ago, before we had kids.* Jill's daughter said, 'Why did we drive all the way here just to sit in the car?' and finally, Jill said, 'Okay, you can swim.'

It *had* just been the Flint question, hadn't it?

Also also also: Once on a work trip to Louisville, she rented a car at the airport. She had to wait in line for twenty minutes. She told the agent, who was a white man, that she wanted satellite radio, and the agent said it would be an extra $15 and Jill said that was a small price to pay for the pleasure of Beyoncé's company and then she and the agent told each other their favorite Beyoncé songs. (Jill's was 'Crazy in Love', and the agent's was 'Irreplaceable').

In the garage, she found the car, stowed her suitcase in its trunk and her purse on the passenger seat, and pulled into the line to exit. There was another wait, of about eight minutes, during which Jill fiddled with the radio and couldn't get the satellite stations to work. When she pulled up to the booth to present her rental papers, she said to the attendant, who was a black woman, 'I asked for satellite radio, but they didn't give it to me.'

With a notable lack of sympathy, the woman said, 'It doesn't work in the garage.'

But it also didn't work when Jill pulled out of the garage. She circled the entire airport and re-entered the rental-car area. She bypassed the lanes where one was supposed to return cars, parked, and approached the booth on foot. She said to the same woman from before, 'I really don't think the satellite radio is activated in my car.'

'Go inside, and they'll give you a different car.'

'Can't you just make it work in the car I already have?' Jill said.

'You need to go inside,' the attendant said.

'I don't want to go back inside,' Jill said. 'I just waited

in line for twenty minutes to get this car. And I specified that I wanted satellite radio.'

'Then call the 1-800 number in your rental agreement.'

'I don't *want* to call a 1-800 number!' Jill shouted. 'I want to be helped by a real human being!'

There was a silence, and then, in a withering tone, the attendant said, 'Ma'am, I am a real human being.'

She and Jill looked at each other. The attendant wore a red polo shirt with the icon of the rental-car company stitched into the fabric above her left breast; her hair was in cornrows, and she was probably about Jill's age.

'Yes,' Jill said, 'I realize that.'

Another silence ensued.

'Do you?' the woman asked.

Jill can't figure out how to access Dave Duncan's Google doc without contacting Dave Duncan himself, but she checks the live cages, all three of them, twice on Christmas Day. She drives by them once before she and her family leave for the movie theater and once after dinner. The cages are all empty. According to Jill's phone, the temperature has fallen to two degrees.

It's on the morning of the twenty-sixth, around 7 a.m., while jogging, that she sees Kiwi again. He's in a yard two doors down from the yard where she saw him before, on Tyler Drive. He's sniffing the base of a tree. This time, Jill suppresses the impulse to call out his name. She stops running when she is still twenty-five feet away. She takes a step onto the wintry lawn closest to her and stands there for a few seconds, then, slowly, she drops to her knees. The ground is so cold! (This morning, the temperature is twelve degrees; she is wearing two pairs of leggings and, on her torso, long underwear, a fleece sweatshirt and a thick jacket).

She considers pulling out her phone and looking at the recommendations from Vanessa that Amy texted her, but Jill is pretty sure she remembers them: *Act like you're hurt. Whimper and moan.*

She lowers her bottom against her heels then lies down on her left side, keeping her ear a few inches off the ground. If Kiwi is aware of her, he gives no sign of it. She whimpers, first briefly and quietly – experimentally – and it comes out sounding, of all things, sexual. She focuses on injecting pain into the whimper – genuine sorrow, real remorse. She grows louder. She draws her knees up, into the fetal position.

How, at Amy's birthday party, did she know they didn't belong there? How did she *know*? And would answering these questions be tolerable or intolerable? What would happen next?

In the winter dawn, she continues whimpering, and at last, Kiwi glances in her direction. He seems nonchalant, possibly disdainful. She whimpers again. She waits to see if he will try to help her or if she will have to help herself.

Creative Differences

The film crew flew in from New York, and the agency people flew in from LA; direct flights to Wichita, it turns out, do not exist from either city. Now the agency people are hanging out at the bar of their mid-level chain hotel (or this is where they were when Ben last saw them) while the film crew, accompanied by Melissa Simon, scouts locations for tomorrow's shoot.

They met Melissa at her apartment, which was an unremarkable one-bedroom – junky furniture, Indian tapestry bedspread – with many of what she confirmed were her own photos pinned to the walls. The four-person crew and Melissa then got in the rental van and, with Ben driving and Melissa in the second row, they passed the bagel place where she said she often works on her laptop during the afternoons. Melissa was enthusiastic about the idea of filming there, to the extent that Ben wondered if friends of hers own the place, and Ben was tasked with conveying that it wasn't quite the right setting. For the last hour, Melissa has been leading them around the campus of the University of Wichita, where, through the Office of Public Affairs, they've already obtained permission to film. It's an overcast afternoon in late March, and the students are on spring break.

On the second floor of a large brick building, she opens a heavy door to reveal a computer lab with dim lighting and beige curtains pulled over the windows. One lone student sits in front of a monitor, earbuds in, simultaneously editing photos on a desktop computer and watching *The Royal Tenenbaums* on a laptop computer; onscreen, Gwyneth Paltrow smokes while wearing heavy eyeliner and a fur coat. 'This is where I spent most of my time as an undergrad,' Melissa says. 'Thrilling, right?'

In addition to Ben, who is the producer, the crew is comprised of Justin, the director; Matthias, the DP; and Ryan, the gaffer. It's unclear to Ben if Melissa knows that Justin is kind of famous; he's made two widely praised feature-length documentaries, the first about a youth orchestra in Afghanistan and the second about fracking in a small town in Virginia. If Melissa had upon shaking hands with Justin proclaimed herself a fan, it would have mildly disgusted him and, Ben is sure, he'd have retracted. But if over the next twenty-four hours it becomes apparent that she really has no idea who he is, Justin will eventually become petulant toward her, offended by her lack of deference. As with nipping in the bud the notion of filming at the bagel place, it is Ben's responsibility to discreetly convey to Melissa Justin's renown.

Melissa is walking in front of them, and whenever she glances back, Ben is struck by the prettiness of her face; whenever she turns away, he is struck by the fact that she's a lot fatter than she appeared either during the Skype calls that occurred a few weeks ago among her, him, Justin and the agency people, or in the photos of her he's seen. She has a trim torso and disproportionately big hips, ass and thighs. And not disproportionately big in a Kim Kardashian sexy way – big in a precursor-of-frumpy-mom way, precursor of his own mother, though Melissa is twenty-four. Ben's assessment is unconnected to any attraction or lack thereof to Melissa – he's gay – and tied strictly to aesthetic implications; Matthias will need to shoot her from the waist up. Or, given the ever-increasing fatness of Americans, and given that Melissa is the project's only Midwesterner and least famous participant, maybe they should take her fatness and, so to speak, run with it? This is a question for Nancy, the agency's broadcast producer, and Ben guesses she'll come down on the side of fat concealment. Nancy, who is fifty, tends to be overtly sexist in a way most men in 2014 no longer are.

They are walking by a storage room, with a kind of concession-stand opening and shelves of photo equipment visible behind locked windows, when Justin says, 'Matthias, what if we shoot her in there, with all the gear behind her? Would you be able to get enough distance to pull focus?'

'You want to shoot me in the cage?' Melissa giggles. 'With, like, literally not one speck of natural light?'

'It'll look cool,' Justin says. 'Trust me.' He says, 'Hey, what's up?' to the broad-shouldered, big-bellied, black-T-shirted man with a salt-and-pepper ponytail sitting at the window, who has glanced up only fleetingly from the screen of his phone. Now, the man regards them quizzically; he is perched on a stool beneath fluorescent lights, and in back of him, the equipment is stacked floor to ceiling: tripods, digital and film cameras, lenses, lighting kits.

'Clarence, I don't know if you remember me,' Melissa says. 'I graduated in 2012? Melissa Simon?' She gestures to the crew. 'These guys are here from New York City filming a documentary that I'm part of, and they want to maybe interview me *here*.'

Clarence's quizzical expression does not change.

'Ben Schneider.' Ben slides a business card through the open window. 'Producer. Would that be cool if we film in there? We have permission from the Public Affairs Office.'

'This is the equipment cage,' Clarence says.

'No, exactly,' Ben says. 'And since Melissa is a photographer, it's like, hey, the subject in her natural habitat.'

'We'll totally respect the gear,' Justin adds. 'Put everything back the way we found it.'

Clarence seems, if anything, more confused. He says, 'You're shooting something for the Public Affairs Office?'

'No, we have permission from the Public Affairs Office,'

Ben says. 'We're making a documentary about American creativity.'

Clarence then calls the Public Affairs Office for confirmation before grudgingly allowing them to invade his domain. When the five of them have followed Justin through the door next to the concession window, Ben sees that the interior of the space is probably ten by eight feet, almost more of a closet than a room. It is, of course, better if the scope of what they're doing – taking over the room for the rest of today and all of tomorrow – dawns on Clarence slowly. But often such people are easily pacified; when Clarence gets hungry, Ben thinks, they can buy him a twelve-inch sub or whatever it is a portly Wichita Cerberus likes to eat.

The first thing that takes a long time is getting room tone, for which Justin wants to turn off the heat for the entire building (it isn't going to happen but nevertheless requires another call to the Public Affairs Office on Ben's part, in the infinitesimal hope that his contact there will call maintenance), then Justin wants to turn off the fluorescent lights, then he wants to unplug a mini-fridge. If they can't get the heat turned off by morning, Ben assures Justin, undoubtedly they can get egg-crate foam tonight at Walmart or Home Depot. Meanwhile, Ryan is doing a lighting check, setting up an LED that Matthias says should be bounced.

Melissa stands by the door, her arms folded, watching them intently. 'What will you be shooting with?' she asks.

No one responds, then Ben says, 'We use a digital cinema camera called a RED Dragon.'

'A Scarlet or a Raven?' Melissa asks.

Justin gives a little snort and says, 'Well, la di da.'

Melissa seems not to take offense. 'I primarily shoot stills,' she says cheerfully, 'but I've played around with video.'

Ben says, 'It's a Raven.'

As Justin and Ryan discuss whether they'll need fill light, Melissa says, 'Ben, where are you from?' If she doesn't know that Justin is famous, she does, apparently, recognize that Ben is not – that despite his producer title, he is her low-level point person. Outside her apartment, just before she climbed into the van, she made a wide-eyed, pleased expression and murmured to him, confidingly, 'This is crazy!' Or maybe it's that she can tell he's gay and therefore she's more comfortable interacting with him than with his slouchily handsome, heterosexually aloof colleagues.

In the equipment room, Ben says, 'I've lived in New York for fifteen years.'

'Really?' Melissa says. 'You're so young-looking. How old are you?'

'I'm thirty-two.'

'Oh, so you're counting when you were in college? Did you go to college in New York?'

'Yes,' he says. 'I went to NYU.'

'Did you start college when you were seventeen?'

Frequently, on the job, Ben thinks, If I were easily annoyed, I'd probably be annoyed right now. Aloud, calmly, he says, 'No, I started college when I was eighteen.

So you're right, I should have said I've lived in New York for fourteen years, not fifteen.'

'Where did you grow up?'

'Delaware. A suburb of Wilmington.' After a pause, he adds, 'Are you from Kansas?'

She shakes her head. 'Sioux City, Iowa. I've been trying to think of what to tell you guys to do while you're here.' Again, she giggles. 'I think maybe Wichita is a better place to live than to visit. But it *is* a great place to be an artist.' There's a confidence with which she says this that Ben finds what – ridiculous? Enviable? He has for four years been working on a documentary of his own, about a blind Cuban septuagenarian in the Bronx, he's even received funding from Sundance, but would he ever casually refer to himself as an artist?

He says to Melissa, 'We're here for the shoot – for you. No worries about tourist attractions.'

Melissa gestures toward the other members of the crew, who are still conferring about the LED. 'Do all of them live in New York?'

'Yes,' Ben says.

'And do you usually work together?' Melissa asks. 'I'm guessing you're freelance?'

Freelance isn't the right term for someone of Justin's stature – he has his own production company – so, on the off-chance he's listening, Ben says, 'I'm freelance, but I work with these guys a lot. Just for this documentary, we've shot the footage for six of the subjects. You're our sixth.'

'Who's left?' Melissa asks.

A kind of bonding often arises on sets from *not* trying hard to get to know one another, not being overtly jovial and inquisitive. The subtext is, we're all busy, we're getting this done as efficiently as possible, but of course even so, during the hours together that aren't really all that efficient, a camaraderie organically asserts itself. Melissa's forced small talk, however – again, it's good Ben isn't easily annoyed.

He says, 'You're our last subject. A film crew on the West Coast has shot the other four.'

'Have you worked with Parkington before?'

'Not personally,' Ben says. 'No.'

The reason they are here, the reason Ben is standing in Wichita, Kansas, talking to Melissa Simon, is toothpaste. Parkington is a multinational maker of personal-care products that hired Kitley & Weiss – it's the K&W folks who are now drinking at the hotel – to create an internet campaign around a brand of toothpaste that has existed for seventy-two years. The campaign will feature artists – yes, in fairness to Melissa, artists – in various mediums, and Justin et al are the ones making the documentary, or six-tenths of it, that will show the artists in their daily lives and highlight their individual talents.

Ironically, it's Justin who would be a more fitting, less surprising subject of the documentary than Melissa. The other artists are an opera singer who's the only living opera singer most Americans have heard of; a best-selling author of legal thrillers; an eleven-year-old who was nominated for a Best Supporting Actress Oscar; a maker of patchwork quilts that depict slave narratives; a former Poet Laureate; a principal dancer with the New York City Ballet; a Broadway actress; and a husband-and-wife folk duo who, between them, play eleven instruments. And then there's Melissa – chubby twenty-four-year-old Midwestern Melissa. She's a photographer, which is to say that two years ago she graduated from the University of Wichita with degrees in both early childhood education and art with a photo media concentration. She currently spends mornings as a preschool teacher, but since graduating, has, rather improbably, made not one but two photo series that went viral.

The first, titled 'Slideshow', featured the children – one child per photo – at the preschool where she works coming down a slide, smiling joyously. The series appeared on an obscure parenting website, then got reproduced in about a million other places. Melissa is white, and all the children in the photos are black; as they drove from the Wichita airport to the hotel, Matthias, who himself is black, remarked that Melissa must have taken the picture of every black kid in Wichita, which prompted Ben to look online at the city's racial demographics (as of 2011, 72 per cent white).

Melissa's second series, which she'd been working on prior to the posting of 'Slideshow', was titled 'Body/Hair'. For a year, each time she performed any act of depilation, she documented it: tweezing her eyebrows while peering in her bathroom mirror; shaving her legs while perched on the side of the tub, her toes near the drain, partially obscured by soap suds, the blades of a candy-colored razor set against her calf; and yes, trimming her pubic hair (light brown, suitably uncomfortable to behold). In Ben's opinion, the photos were neither artful nor sexy – and he doubts a straight man would beg to differ – but worst of all, they'd been poorly color-corrected. Of course, only an idiot thinks viral popularity is indicative of quality, and the series was a hit particularly among women; apparently it was the wife of the Parkington CEO who suggested Melissa for inclusion in the toothpaste campaign.

'Do you travel internationally for jobs?' Melissa is asking now. 'Or do you stay in the US?'

Before Ben can answer, Justin says to him, 'Can you check what time sunrise is? I wonder if we should get B-roll of her walking around campus with the sun coming up, even before we shoot in here.'

Simultaneously, Ben says, 'Actually, the call time tomorrow is 12:30,' and Melissa says, 'I work in the morning.'

Justin gives her a look that's almost flirtatious. 'You can't get the day off?' Justin's attractiveness is of the stubbly, swollen-lipped, dark-haired bed-head variety, and he is, for the first time in Melissa's presence, deploying it.

Which makes it slightly surprising when Melissa firmly says, 'Unfortunately, no.' Could she also be queer?

'What's your job?' Justin asks. 'Want Ben to call your boss?'

'Justin,' Ben says. 'We can make her schedule work.' As it happens, the real celebrities were more flexible with their time – the opera singer gave them two eighteen-hour days, one at the opera house and one at her apartment, *and* she cooked seafood curry for the entire crew. To Melissa, Ben says, 'You have no hard out tomorrow night, correct?'

'Yes,' Melissa says. 'Correct.' She looks at Justin. 'I teach preschool.'

'Oh, yeah,' Justin says. 'Your Mary Poppins gig. How could I forget?' Switching to his warmest voice yet, he says, 'All righty. This is how we'll do it.' Because conceding doesn't come easily to him, good-naturedly conceding Justin, as opposed to peevishly conceding Justin, is the most charming Justin of all. 'We'll meet here at 12:30. I mean, come earlier if you can. That would be awesome. But starting at 12:30 at the latest, we'll shoot for a couple hours in here. I'll be off-camera, asking you questions. It'll be a zoo with all the K&W people, but just treat them like static. Ben will be the one running interference, and all you need to do is focus on my questions and be yourself. After the interview, we'll get some B-roll of you walking around campus, driving your car, all that good stuff. Then we'll stop back at your apartment to get you brushing your teeth, although we'll also do that in one of the bathrooms here, to keep our options open. Oh, and Ben talked to you about bringing some prints from your two series, right? We want to get close-ups of the photos with your hands.'

'That sounds fine,' Melissa says. 'But the brushing-my-teeth part – you're kidding, right?'

Ben and Justin make eye contact. She wants to know if Justin is kidding? Is *she* kidding?

With deliberate calmness, Ben says, 'All the artists have done it for the documentary.'

Melissa looks amused, but incredulously so. 'You're telling me that you filmed Beatrice Chisolm brushing her teeth? And Jack and Lulu?'

Again, Ben and Justin make eye contact; Matthias and Ryan, who were previously talking, have also gone silent and are observing the exchange, and even Clarence seems to be listening.

'Yes,' Ben says. 'We did.'

'Dude, it's in the contract,' Justin says. 'Did you read the contract?'

Still seeming unpleasantly amused, Melissa says, 'After I brush my teeth, do I turn to the camera and say, "Wow! White Sparkle toothpaste sure is effective!"?'

Her sarcasm and its abruptness are unsettling. Although Ben met her in person just over an hour ago, he's been talking to her one-on-one and during group Skype calls with the agency for six weeks. The initial Skyping was her unacknowledged audition, a means of determining how attractive and charismatic she was. Sufficiently attractive and sufficiently charismatic were the answers, at least when she was seated at a desk that obscured the lower half of her body. But during none of the exchanges did Ben see evidence of this abrasive streak.

'Seriously,' Justin says. 'Did you read the contract? It's all laid out.'

'Yeah,' Melissa says. 'I read it. But it's, like, sixteen pages. And the language in it – I'm not a lawyer.'

'Well, it's all in there, my friend,' Justin says.

'You know what?' Melissa says. 'I finally understand.' She looks between Ben and Justin. 'This is a commercial. I should have realized it. None of you have ever used the word *commercial* with me. You keep using the word *documentary*, you keep saying it's a documentary about creativity being underwritten by Parkington. And I'm so dumb I've believed you.' She's gazing only at Justin as she says, 'I didn't think you'd direct a commercial.'

So she does know who Justin is. But it would seem that she doesn't know that Justin has directed commercials for, among other products, athletic shoes, luxury cars and a telecommunications conglomerate. It was five years ago, on a car-commercial shoot, that Ben and Justin met.

Melissa glances among them. 'Do you guys know how much I'm being paid for this?'

No one responds.

'Five hundred dollars,' she says. 'You're paying me five hundred dollars to make a commercial for a huge corporation.'

'What do you think union scale is?' Justin says.

'I'm lucky to be included, right? Because I'm the one nobody's ever heard of? But throughout this whole process, ever since you first contacted me, Ben, and during the Skype calls – there was something weird about how you all acted, and only now do I realize what it was. The weirdness isn't that you were trying to get me to be in a commercial for toothpaste. The weirdness is that you were trying to get me to be in a commercial while pretending you weren't.'

'Melissa,' Ben says. 'You're an incredibly talented photographer, and this campaign will get your name and your work in front of a global audience. If you feel like you're not being fairly compensated, I can follow up with K&W and ask for more. We aren't the ones who decided on your payment. But we definitely want you to feel good about this experience. This really is meant to be a fun, cool project celebrating artists and creativity.'

Melissa laughs an ugly laugh. The question now isn't whether her previous giggly question-asking was fake but what per cent fake it was. Oddly, knowing that not only is the chipper demeanor not the totality of her personality, but that she employs it strategically, just as she photographs her own body strategically – it makes Ben respect and even like her more.

Slowly, she says, 'I don't think I want to do this. I don't want to be in your—' She makes air quotes, ' "documentary".'

'Are you fucking kidding me?' Justin says.

'Hey,' Ben says to Justin. 'Why don't Melissa and I go get coffee and you guys can keep scouting?' He turns to Melissa. 'Want to get coffee?'

They go to the student center, a six-minute walk. As soon as they've parted ways with the rest of the crew, she reverts to being nice again, not acerbic. She orders green tea, and he orders a decaf espresso, and after they sit, she says, 'I did read the contract. I really did. I think I even remember the sentence now. Was it something about agreeing to cooperate with reasonable promotion of the Parkington brand? Because I thought that meant I couldn't be in the documentary and then, like, slander something Parkington makes. Like I couldn't tweet that their laundry detergent sucks.'

'I didn't write your contract,' Ben says. 'Here's what I care about. What can I do to make you feel comfortable with the shoot tomorrow?'

She is quiet, seeming to ponder the question. At last, she says, 'If you'd said, "We're making a commercial for toothpaste and we want you to be in it," I'd probably have said yes. That's the irony. It's not like I think I'm too good to sell out. But you tricked me.'

'I get where you're coming from,' Ben says. 'But I wonder if this is partly an issue of semantics. There just aren't such clear demarcations anymore between commercial and documentary content, especially online.'

She raises her eyebrows. 'Really? That's really what you believe?'

'Like I said, I get where you're coming from. I don't want you to think I don't.'

'Or if this actually was a documentary and you were paying me nothing – that would have been fine, too. I never thought people got paid to be in documentaries anyway.'

She's right – they usually don't – but he doesn't affirm her statement.

'Honestly, when "Slideshow" went viral,' she says, 'I felt uncomfortable. Should I have paid the kids whose pictures I took? But also, *I* didn't make any money. The original website that ran the photos didn't pay me, and then literally hundreds of other publications just helped themselves. I didn't know that was legal. In the end, I was paid a grand total of fifty Euros from some random Dutch magazine, which came out to I think sixty-six American dollars.'

'That's a huge bummer,' he says. 'Photo copyright these days is like the Wild West. Almost no one understands the work by people like you that goes into the images.'

'I told myself, Melissa, just enjoy this success and attention that's probably once in a lifetime. Then, a few months later, my shaving pictures got even more attention. And I felt weird about those, too. As a feminist, for one thing, and also I was like, Has the entire world really just seen my pubes? Who will ever date me now?' When Ben laughs, she says, 'I'm not joking. I know there's this idea, with social media and everything, that we all want as much attention as possible, all the time, but one of the things about my early success that's been eye-opening is that I've gotten so much attention and it doesn't feel that great. It feels strange. That's helped me realize that my goal isn't to find the biggest audience. It's to be able to keep taking pictures and to find an audience who really appreciates what I do.'

My early success. An audience who really appreciates what

I do. Her confidence! It's so bizarrely pure, so uncompetitive. Should Ben move to Wichita?

'Can I ask you a question?' she says. 'How much is Justin getting paid for this?'

'I truly don't know. But he's not a good frame of comparison because he's directing six of the shoots for the documentary.'

'But, like, what's the range? If you had to guess?'

'If you're asking if it's more than five hundred dollars, sure.' If he had to guess, $100,000. He considers saying $10,000, but what if even that sounds high to her? 'It's just really hard to know,' he says. 'Plus, he has an agent.'

'I'm sure you won't tell me,' she says, 'but how much are you getting paid?'

'If this is about the money, I'm confident we can get you more. The exposure, though – you can't put a price on that.'

'At the rate I'm going, I'll be forty-five when I pay off my student loans,' she says. 'Literally. I calculated. And I wish I could get an MFA in photo, but then what? I'll be dead without paying off my loans.'

'I have student loans,' he says. 'I know. It sucks.' The truth is that most people in the documentary field don't. They don't seem so different from you, with their shitty apartments and their roommates and their artsy hustling, then it turns out their parents have a summer house on Martha's Vineyard (Justin), or the way they met their agent is that he was their Harvard roommate's uncle (Matthias).

Melissa says, 'It's just, what you keep saying about payment and exposure – why do I have to decide between them?'

'No, right. You shouldn't. You don't.' He is not entirely sure why, in this moment, he says, 'For what it's worth, I'm working on a documentary, too. I'm directing one. I get the whole blood, sweat and tears thing.'

'What's yours about?'

'A Cuban guy in his seventies. He left when Castro came to power, went back to fight in the Bay of Pigs, was sent to a Cuban prison for six months after the US threw all those guys under the bus, went blind due to being tortured, then he was released back to the US in '62. He ends up working as a cab dispatcher, getting married and having five sons.'

'Wow.'

'I'm just scared he'll die before I can finish. I need to buckle down.' Quickly, Ben adds, 'Not to sound like an asshole. Obviously, it would be sad for his family if he died. And for him. Not just for me.'

She smiles. 'I knew what you meant. What's his name?'

'Diego Ruiz.' Ben pauses. 'A lot of the time, I'm, like, why the fuck am I doing this? Making a documentary is expensive, it's a pain in the ass, I'm calling in favors from my friends. But Diego is amazing. He wears dark glasses, he has this huge belly, and he's hilarious. He's been through some of the worst things that can happen to a person, and he's warm and funny and loves his family.

And for some reason he's trusting me to help tell his story. I know it sounds corny, but it's a privilege.'

Divulging all this – it really wasn't calculated on Ben's part. It was true. Is this why it works? She says, 'Yeah, exactly. You know in the story of "Rumpelstiltskin", how the miller's daughter spins straw into gold? That's what I feel like making art is.' Then she says, 'If you can try to get me more money, I'd really appreciate it. But whatever. I'll be there tomorrow at 12:30.'

That night, when Ben and Ryan return to the hotel from buying egg-crate foam at Walmart, a massive amount of barbecue, procured by a K&W assistant, has been laid out buffet-style in the part of the lobby where the continental breakfast will be served tomorrow morning: pulled pork, ribs, brisket, as well as coleslaw, fries, and mac and cheese. Even though the hotel's modest-sized bar is right there, the crew and the eight agency people keep drinking in the lobby after dinner, while the mac and cheese congeals and the meat grows old. The girl behind the front desk, who looks like an undergrad, does nothing to indicate they should go elsewhere.

On the plane ride out, Ben decided he'd have no more than two beers tonight, but Justin is drinking a lot, so pretty soon Ben has had four. Although Justin is married to a dark-haired, incredibly beautiful woman from Venezuela, a model, three times on location when Justin and Ben were both very drunk, Ben gave Justin blow jobs; the third time, Justin also gave Ben a blow job. Ben is happy to get drunk if he and Justin are going to hook up, but he doesn't want to not hook up *and* be hungover tomorrow.

He has just opened his fifth beer when Nancy, the broadcast producer, perches on the arm of the couch where he's sitting, sets a hand on his shoulder and says, 'I hear our ingénue got stage fright today.'

'It's under control,' Ben says.

Nancy smiles tightly, though it's difficult to discern if the tightness is due to her mood or to the work she's had done. 'Keep it that way,' she says.

But he's already received the text from Melissa; he received it at 8:56 p.m. and he just didn't know it for a half hour because he didn't feel his phone vibrate. The text says: 'Ben I thought about it and I changed my mind again. I don't want to appear in the documentary/commercial/whatever. This is definite. Sorry for any confusion.'

By this point, a garrulous medical-device sales rep named Randy, in town from San Antonio, Texas, has joined the gathering in the lobby, and everyone is tipsy enough to be tickled rather than annoyed. Ben walks outside to the parking lot to call Melissa. He must stand several feet from the entrance to avoid setting off the automatic doors.

'What's going on?' he says when she answers. 'I got your text.'

'I just feel too weird about everything,' she says. 'I know I wouldn't be able to relax during the shoot tomorrow and give you the footage you need.'

'Let us worry about that. I appreciate your consideration, but that's our job.'

'I'm not doing it,' she says. 'I don't want to waste more of your time.' Her voice is neither tentative, as it initially was in their encounters, nor caustic, as it was later. She does in fact sound resolute, but more soberly so than angrily.

He says, 'What can I do to change your mind?'

After a beat, she says, 'When we were having coffee, you were convincing. You seemed like a sincerely nice person, not a condescending New Yorker who thinks it's hilarious he's in Kansas, and maybe you really are nice. But after I got home today, I was thinking about your documentary about the Cuban guy. *You* know the difference between a documentary and a commercial. And you're the person who first got in touch with me – you're the one who said from the start it was a documentary. I don't know what instructions you got from the Kitley & Weiss people, but you could have told me the truth.'

'It feels like we're going in circles here,' he says. 'How can we move forward? We want to do right by you, Melissa.'

'See, I think you might actually believe what you're saying. I think maybe you're so used to working in this fake way that you don't even recognize it. But I know you won't care if I come off looking good or bad tomorrow. All you care about is getting me to do whatever you've already decided I should do on-camera.'

'I can give you my word we have no interest in making you look bad.'

'Your word?' She chortles.

'What if we don't film you brushing your teeth?' he says. 'We just do the interview?'

It immediately occurs to him that this isn't his bargaining chip to offer, so he's a bit relieved when she says, 'No.'

'Well, if it makes any difference,' he says, 'I talked to the agency folks, and they can raise your fee to $2,500.' He hasn't talked to anyone yet – he's been too preoccupied with Justin and blow jobs – but he's confident he can get this amount. Possibly he could get her more, but if he gets too much, it will emphasize how they lowballed her at first. He says, 'I don't know what you pay on your student loans, but for me, that's about eight months' worth.'

She's quiet again, and he can tell that it does make a difference. But it makes a difference in the sense that it's harder to turn down the additional money, not that it changes her mind. She says, 'No. And I have to get up early for work, so please don't call or text me again.'

Of course Nancy insists on calling her. First, Nancy freaks out in the lobby – she says, 'It's a fucking hostage situation, and she's the hostage *and* the terrorist' – then she goes outside with Ben to call Melissa from Ben's phone. It's almost 10 o'clock and maybe 40 degrees, and they're not wearing coats. At Nancy's instruction, Ben puts Melissa on speaker, though it's Nancy who's doing most of the talking.

'This isn't coastal elites trying to deceive you,' Nancy says. 'This is the career opportunity of a fucking lifetime dropping in your lap. Besides which, how could we have tricked you about the nature of what we're doing when you had umpteen conference calls with one of the most famous ad agencies in the world?'

Melissa says nothing.

'Honey, do you know where I grew up?' Nancy asks. 'I'm from Wentzville, Missouri. I'm practically your next door neighbor. And you know what? I may have lived in LA for thirty years, but I'm still Jenny from the block.' Ben winces; he hopes Melissa is too young to get the reference.

'Whether you want to stay in Wichita or move to New York, LA, or for that matter Kansas City, being part of a project of this prestige is your calling card,' Nancy continues. 'I'm telling you, woman to woman, Midwesterner to Midwesterner, that there's absolutely no question this exposure is in your best interest.'

The silence from Melissa lasts long enough that Ben wonders if she ended the call. Then, quietly, she says, 'I don't want exposure.'

'Oh, for Christ's sake,' Nancy says. 'Do you know how many people came here for tomorrow's shoot? Thirteen. Thirteen! Do you know how much it costs to fly out that many people, for the hotel, the equipment, the man hours? And because you have cold feet, because you're too precious to be filmed sticking a goddamn toothbrush in your mouth, you think we're flushing $60,000 in expenses down the toilet? That's not how it works, sweetheart. You signed a contract. We'll see you tomorrow.'

'No, actually—' Melissa's voice grows marginally louder. 'I never signed the contract. I wasn't playing hardball. I was planning to ask you about this, Ben, because there's a line where I'm supposed to sign it and right under, there's a line where my agent is supposed to sign, but I don't have an agent, so I wasn't sure what to do. And I may not be a lawyer, but I know enough to know that if I didn't sign the contract—' She doesn't say the rest.

In the dark hotel parking lot, Nancy glares at Ben. Yes, this is his fuck-up. But, in his defense, getting the contract was on his to-do list for tomorrow; subjects often don't sign until the day, and sometimes until weeks after.

'You know what you are?' Nancy says, and it's not clear if she's speaking to Melissa, Ben, or both of them. 'You're an entitled little millennial piece of shit.'

The toothpaste campaign is an enormous, unequivocal success. Relatively few people see the full documentary, but the ninety-second montage of the artists brushing their teeth, which never airs on television, is viewed 52 million times on YouTube. Why is it so enjoyable to watch somewhat famous people brush their teeth? Ben spends a fair amount of time pondering this question (he himself watches the montage repeatedly even after his involvement with Parkington is complete) and concludes that it's because teeth-brushing is universal. It's personal but not excessively so – the participants seem like good sports rather than exhibitionists – and it's real. Using White Sparkle is of course beside the point; everyone in the video does actually brush their teeth. Even people who hire others to do mundane tasks for them, even the opera singer – such people still brush their own teeth.

That night in Wichita, after he and Nancy re-entered the hotel lobby and broke the news about Melissa's change of heart, everyone disbanded quickly, with varying levels of irritation and outright rage. But it wasn't as if any of them personally lost money. Parkington was paying K&W, and K&W was paying the crew, and they didn't end up replacing Melissa. They just included nine subjects in the documentary instead of ten.

The two calls to Melissa from the parking lot had so thoroughly soured the night – the whole trip – that the question of whether Ben and Justin would hook up was rendered moot. But then, because Ben gave up on willing it to happen, it did happen after all. As they were riding up in the elevator, Justin conveyed a kind of unspoken sleepy-eyed receptivity that coexisted with, or ran beneath, his overtly expressed contempt for Melissa. But after Ben gave him a blow job, Justin didn't reciprocate, which wouldn't have felt as bad if he'd never done it before; it would have felt like standard-issue quasi-straight guy bullshit instead of a regression of intimacy.

Ben occasionally Googles Melissa Simon. He half-expects to hear from or about her, at the least in the form of another viral slideshow, but a few years pass without this happening. Based on what he can infer from LinkedIn, she does go to grad school but not for photography – she gets a master's degree in, of all things, business adminis-tration. And on Instagram, she seems to be dating, then married to, a tubby, smiley guy named Mikey.

Ben makes a trailer of his existing footage of Diego Ruiz

to secure more funding. But after three years, when he hears from the eldest Ruiz son that their father died a month before, Ben has shot 150 additional hours of footage and watched zero of them. Oddly, upon learning of Diego's death, Ben feels the temptation to relay the news to Melissa. He doesn't, though, because there's no good reason why he would.

Show Don't Tell

At some point, a rich old man named Ryland W. Peaslee had made an enormous donation to the program, and this was why not only the second-year fellowships he'd endowed but also the people who received them were called Peaslees. You'd say, 'He's a Peaslee,' or 'She's a Peaslee.' Each year, four were granted. There were other kinds of fellowships, but none of them provided as much money – eighty-eight hundred dollars – as the Peaslees. Plus, with all the others, you still had to teach undergrads.

Our professors and the program administrators were cagey about the exact date when we'd receive the letters specifying our second-year funding, but a rumor was going around that it would be on a Monday in mid-March, which meant that, instead of sitting at my desk, I spent most of a morning and an early afternoon standing at the front window of my apartment, scanning the street for the mailman. For lunch, I ate a bowl of Grape-Nuts and yogurt – Monday nights after seminar were when I drank the most, and therefore when life seemed the most charged with flirtatious possibility, so I liked to eat light on those days – then I brushed my teeth, took a shower, and got dressed. It was still only two o'clock. Seminar started at four, and my apartment was a ten-minute walk from campus. I lived on the second floor of a small, crappy Dutch Colonial, on the same street as a bunch of sororities and the co-op, where I occasionally splurged on an organic pineapple, which I'd eat in its entirety. I was weirdly adept at cutting a pineapple, and doing so made me feel like a splendid tropical queen with no one to witness my splendor. It was 1998, and I was twenty-five.

I was so worked up about the funding letter that I decided to pack my bag and wait outside for the mailman, even though the temperature wasn't much above freezing. I sat in the mint-green steel chair on the front stoop, opened the paperback novel I was in the middle of, and proceeded to read not more than a few sentences. Graduate school was the part of my life when I had the most free time and the fewest obligations, when I discussed fiction the most and read it the least. But it was hard to focus when you were, like a pupa, in the process of becoming yourself.

My downstairs neighbor, Lorraine, emerged from her apartment while I was sitting on the stoop, a lit cigarette in her hand; presumably, she'd heard my door open and close and thought that I had left. We made eye contact, and I smirked – involuntarily, if that mitigates things, which it probably doesn't. She started to speak, but I held up my palm, standing as I did so, and shook my head. Then I pulled my bag onto my shoulder and began walking toward campus.

Lorraine was in her early fifties, and she had moved to the Midwest the same week in August that I had, also to get a master's degree but in a different department; she told me she was writing a memoir. I'd moved from Philadelphia, and she'd moved from Santa Fe. She was dark-haired and wore jeans and turquoise jewelry – I had the impression that she was more of a reinvented Northeastern WASP than a real desert dweller – and was solicitous in a way that made me wary. I wanted to have torrid affairs with hot guys my age, not hang out with a fifty-two-year-old woman. In early September, after sleeping at Doug's apartment for the first time, I'd returned home around eight in the morning, hungover and delighted with myself, and she'd been sitting on the front stoop, drinking coffee, and I'd said good morning and she'd said, 'How are you?' and I'd said, 'Fine, how are you?' and she'd said, 'I'm thinking about how the English language lacks an adequate vocabulary for grief.' After briefly hesitating, I'd said, 'I guess that's true. Have a nice day!' Then I'd hurried inside.

It was likely because I was distracted by Doug, and our torridness, that I hadn't paid much attention at first to Lorraine's smoking. I could smell the smoke from my apartment, and one day I even pulled out my lease, to check if it specified that smoking wasn't permitted either inside or out – it did – but then I didn't do anything about it.

In the fourth week that Doug and I were dating, his work and mine were discussed in seminar on the same day. Mine was discussed mostly favorably and his was discussed mostly unfavorably, neither of which surprised me. The night before, while naked in Doug's bed, we'd decided to give each other feedback ahead of time. As he lay on top of me, he said that he liked my story, except that he'd been confused by the beginning. I then delivered a seventeen-minute monologue about all the ways he could improve his, at the conclusion of which he stood up, went into the other room, and turned on the TV, even though we hadn't had sex. I believed that a seventeen-minute critique was an act of love, and the truth is that I still do, but the difference between who I was then and who I am now is that now I never assume that anyone I encounter shares my opinion about anything.

The next night, most people went to the bar after class; it was only eight o'clock when Doug said that he had a headache and was going home. I said, 'But getting criticism is why we're in the program, right?' He said, 'Having a headache has nothing to do with the criticism.' Three hours later, leaving the bar, I walked to his apartment. I knocked on his door until he opened it, wearing boxers, a T-shirt and an irked expression. He said, 'I don't really feel like company tonight,' and I said, 'Can't I at least sleep here? We don't have to do it. I know you' – I made air quotes – 'have a headache.'

'You know what, Ruthie? This isn't working.'

I was astonished. 'Are you breaking up with me?'

'Obviously, we jumped into things too fast,' he said. 'So better to correct now than let the situation fester.'

'I don't think "fester" is the word you mean,' I said. 'Unless you see us as an infected wound.'

He glared. 'Don't workshop me.'

It's not that I wasn't deeply upset; it was just that being deeply upset didn't preclude my remarking on his syntax. I walked to my own apartment, and I spent a lot of the next week crying, while intermittently seeing Doug from a few feet away in class and at lectures and bars.

Also during that week, I knocked on Lorraine's door and told her that I could smell her cigarette smoke in my apartment and was respectfully requesting that she smoke elsewhere. She was apologetic, and later that day she left a card and a single sunflower outside my front door – when I saw the sunflower, I was thrilled, because I thought it was from Doug – and, judging from the smell, she continued to smoke enthusiastically. I left a note for her saying that I appreciated the flower but would be contacting our land-lord if she didn't stop. On Saturday, I returned home at one in the morning to find her sitting outside in the mint-green chair, enjoying a cigarette; I suspect that she'd thought I was asleep. She giggled and said, 'This is awkward,' and I ignored her and went inside. The next day, I e-mailed our landlord. After that, I'm pretty sure that Lorraine neither smoked as much on the property nor completely stopped, and I continued to ignore her. That is, I said no actual words to her, though, if she said hello, I nodded my head in acknowledgment.

Another month passed, and one afternoon a commercial airplane crashed in North Carolina, killing all forty-seven passengers and crew members. The next day, Lorraine was sitting in the mint-green chair reading the newspaper when I left the apartment, and she said, 'Have you heard about the plane crash?' and I said, 'Yes,' and kept walking, and I had made it about ten feet when she said, 'You're a fucking bitch.' I was so surprised that I turned around and started laughing. Then I turned around again and walked away.

Once more, a single sunflower appeared outside my door, along with another note: 'That outburst is not who I am. I admire you a lot.' I had already repeated to my classmates the story of my middle-aged turquoise-jewelry-wearing neighbor telling me I was a fucking bitch, and the note left me queasy and disappointed. In the next five months, right up to the afternoon that I was waiting for my funding letter, I interacted with Lorraine as little as possible.

It was, obviously, a reflection of how agitated the funding had made me that I'd sat on the stoop. As I walked to town, I began composing in my head a new e-mail to my landlord. I would, I decided, use the word 'carcinogenic'.

Because there were still ninety minutes before seminar, I stopped at the bookstore. I ran into a classmate named Harold, who had recently said in seminar that everything I wrote gave off the vibe of ten-year-old girls at a slumber party. In the store, Harold told me that the funding letters weren't arriving today. His mail had already been delivered, and so had that of a guy named Cyrus, who lived next door; neither of them had received letters, and the newest intelligence was that the letters would be sent on Wednesday and probably arrive Thursday. Then Harold held up a paperback of *Mao II* and said, 'If DeLillo isn't the ombudsman of American letters right now, I'm at a loss as to who is.'

'I've never actually read him,' I said. Harold's expression turned disapproving, and I added, 'Lend me that when you're finished and I will.'

'It's not mine,' Harold said. 'I just come in here and read twenty pages at a time. But seriously, Ruthie – not even *White Noise?*'

On Friday, a guy in his forties who wasn't famous to the general population but had a cult following among my classmates and me – a distinction I didn't then understand – was coming to speak, and some second-years who lived in a house across the river were hosting the after-party. The funding letters *still* hadn't arrived, or at least this was what I thought when I met my friend Dorothy for dinner at 5:30 at a Thai restaurant; we were eating early so that we could get good seats at the event, which would take place in a campus auditorium. But, when I sat down, Dorothy said, 'I got a Franklin. Did you get a Peaslee? I'll set aside my jealousy and be happy for you if you did.'

In fact, I hadn't received any mail at all, after another exhausting day of stalking the mailman. When I told Dorothy this, I added, 'Or do you think Lorraine stole my letter?'

'Yeah, probably,' Dorothy said.

'No, really,' I said.

'No,' Dorothy said. 'I bet it's there right now. Should we skip dinner and go see?'

Even though I'd left my apartment fifteen minutes before, I considered it. Then I said, 'I've wasted this entire week waiting, and I'm sure I didn't get a Peaslee anyway. But if I don't check I can pretend I got one until after the party tonight. Like Schrödinger's cat.'

'Ha,' Dorothy said, then her features twisted, her eyes filled, and she said, 'I don't mind teaching Comp next year, but the past few weeks have just been such a mind-fuck. It's like a referendum on our destinies.' I adored Dorothy, and her eyes filled with tears in my presence several times a day, and probably several times out of it, too. A lot of the people in our program were nakedly emotional in a way that, in childhood, I had so successfully trained myself not to be that I almost really wasn't. Before entering grad school, I had never felt normal, but here I was competent and well adjusted to a boring degree. I always showed up for class. I met deadlines. I made eye contact. Of course I was chronically sad, and of course various phobias lay dormant inside me, but none of that was currently dictating my behavior. I also didn't possess a certain kind of feral charisma or mystery, and I didn't know, though I wondered a lot, if charisma correlated with talent. That's why Dorothy was right, that funding *did* feel like a referendum.

In the auditorium, Dorothy and I found seats toward the front, next to Jeff and Bhadveer, whom we referred to, unbeknownst to them, as our fake boyfriends. Jeff was tall and plump, and Bhadveer was medium height and skinny, and the four of us were all single and hung out often. In lieu of a greeting, Jeff said, 'I'm not going to ask what funding you guys got, and I don't want you to ask me, and, if it's something you feel compelled to discuss, go sit somewhere else.' Dorothy had entered the row before me and she glanced back and raised her eyebrows, and I mouthed, '*Rhetoric?*' and she nodded. This was the worst funding, besides none, which a handful of students did in fact receive. Or maybe Rhetoric was even worse than nothing, because, if you got nothing, you could find another job, but with Rhetoric you had to teach five days a week for sixty-four hundred dollars a year. Aloud, Dorothy and I said, 'Sure,' and, 'No, that's cool.'

The auditorium filled, which meant that about five hundred people turned out to hear the man with the cult following, who was a graduate of the program. He was wearing an untucked shirt, baggy jeans, and beat-up hiking boots, and halfway through his reading, when he stumbled over a line he had written a decade earlier, he said, 'Fuck, man, I need a drink,' and about seven minutes after that a guy from my program passed a six-pack of beer up onto the stage, and the man yanked off a can, popped it open, and guzzled. He said, 'That's the stuff,' and the audience applauded enthusiastically. I found the man brilliant and wrote down three of his insights, but the beer bit made me uncomfortable in ways it would take between two days and twelve years to pinpoint.

After the talk, in the building's crowded lobby, I was

standing with Jeff when I spotted Lorraine about twenty feet away. 'Eek,' I said. 'Can I hide behind you? I see my weirdo neighbor.'

'The smoker?' Jeff asked.

'Yeah, it's that woman in the black leather trenchcoat.'

'The smoker is Lorraine? She tutors with me at the Writing Center. She's kind of bonkers.'

'Exactly.'

'You know about her daughter, right?'

'Should I?'

'She had a teenage daughter who died of anorexia. And not even that long ago – like two years?'

'Jesus,' I said. 'Maybe I *am* a fucking bitch.'

'After that, I'd smoke, too.'

'I already said I feel bad.' There was a pause – the lobby was still crowded and buzzing – and I said, 'Obviously, that's a horrible tragedy. But aren't her daughter's death and her blowing smoke into my apartment completely separate?'

Jeff shrugged. 'Maybe not to her.'

There had been some question as to whether the after-party would still happen, in light of so many people mourning their second-year funding, but word circulated in the auditorium lobby that it was on. Before we walked over, Dorothy, Jeff, Bhadveer and I stopped at a convenience store.

'I'm not drinking tonight,' I told Dorothy.

She was closing the glass door of a refrigerator, and she frowned and said, 'Why not?'

It was the way that the man with the cult following

had opened the beer onstage combined with my new knowledge of Lorraine's daughter, and I would have told Dorothy this under different circumstances – I told her everything – but it seemed like too much to get into, with Jeff and Bhadveer waiting at the cash register. I said, 'So I don't throw myself at Doug.'

'But if you don't drink you won't throw yourself at anyone else, either.'

'Let's hope,' I said. Doug and I had barely spoken since the first week of October. Following our breakup, we'd communicated only through typed critiques of each other's work – our professor required the critiques to be typed – and Doug's to me were one intellectually distant paragraph under which he wrote, 'Best, Doug,' which always made me think, How can someone who came inside me sign his critiques 'Best'? My critique to him after our breakup was three single-spaced pages, and, in the sense that my comments concerned his story, they were impersonal, but in the sense that his story was autobiographical and he knew that I knew this – he'd told me about the fishing trip with his stepfather that it was based on – they were not impersonal. ('I think this would be a lot more compelling if the protagonist showed greater self-awareness and took responsibility for his role in the boat sinking.') After that, I didn't write him any critiques. I wasn't going to knowingly give him bad advice, but I didn't want to bestow on him another act of love. Or I *did* want to bestow on him acts of love – all I wanted was to bestow – but it was too painful to do so when my ability to edit his work was probably the thing he liked and hated most about me. Also, he'd begun dating an undergraduate named Brianna.

It was dark out, and on the bridge across the river I ended up walking next to Bhadveer, about fifteen feet behind Dorothy and Jeff. 'Can you fucking believe it about Larry?' Bhadveer asked.

'Wait, is Larry a Peaslee?'

'Yeah. Remember that piece of shit he wrote about the Nazi soldier?'

'And who else is one?' I asked.

'You mean besides the guy who has two thumbs and loves blow jobs?' Bhadveer had made fists and was pointing with his thumbs at his face.

'*You* got one?' I said.

'If you're trying to conceal your surprise, try a little harder. Did you get one?'

'I haven't actually seen today's mail, but I doubt it.'

'I bet you were in the running,' he said, which seemed both chivalrous and like something he wouldn't have said if he weren't a recipient.

'Thanks for the vote of confidence.'

'Well, at least one Peaslee has to be female, right?' he said. 'And there aren't that many of you.' This was true. Of our cohort of twenty-two, seven were girls or women or whatever we were supposed to call ourselves and one another – I myself was inconsistent on this front.

I said, 'So you, Larry, and two we don't know.'

———

Program parties were often weird – sometimes they took place at a farmhouse that a group of students rented a few miles out of town, and sometimes attendees did acid, so it wasn't that uncommon for, say, a twenty-three-year-old poet who had grown up in San Francisco and graduated from Brown to be found wandering in his underwear in a frozen cornfield – and I could tell as soon as we arrived that this party was going to be extra weird. A second-year named Chuck was standing by the front door, holding a Pez dispenser topped by a skull, and as people entered he offered them a candy, saying, as it landed in their palms, 'Memento mori.' By some mixture of intuition and strategic-ally looking around, I knew immediately that neither the man with the cult following nor Doug was there.

In the kitchen, as Dorothy waited to set her six-pack in the refrigerator, the girl-woman in front of her, whose name was Cecilia, abruptly whirled around and hissed, 'Can you please get the fuck out of my space bubble?'

Dorothy and I joined a conversation in progress among five people, and it soon emerged that one of them, Jonah, was the third Peaslee. Jonah's mother had starred in a popular night-time soap opera in the eighties, and, to a one, Jonah's stories featured autoerotic asphyxiation, which I'd been unfamiliar with and had to have explained to me by Dorothy. But Jonah's autoerotic-asphyxiation descriptions were artful, and the news that he was a Peaslee didn't offend my sense of justice.

The group of us speculated about who the fourth Peaslee was, and the consensus was Aisha, who was one of two black people in the entire program, and who was in her late thirties and had formerly been an anesthesiologist. She rarely came to parties, which I respected. I couldn't stay away from them – what if something juicy happened and/or Doug was in the mood to reunite? It was also technically possible that the fourth Peaslee was a woman named Marcy, who was in her early thirties, married, and had a two-year-old kid who was always sick. However, it was widely understood that Marcy was a terrible writer; more than once, I'd heard the suggestion that her acceptance into the program had been a clerical error.

I was in the living room, perched side by side on a windowsill with Bhadveer, when three girl-women converged in a group hug that lasted, and I'm not exaggerating, five minutes. These were the only women in my year besides me, Dorothy, Aisha and Marcy. There was a fair amount of space around them, so that everyone along the room's periphery bore witness to the hug, which I assumed was part of the point. In the first few seconds of the hug, I thought, okay, for sure none of you are Peaslees, which gave credence to the Aisha theory – or could it be me? Was there any chance? *Should* I leave to go check my mail? – and as the hug approached the thirty-second mark I thought, For God's sake, we get it, you're strong females who support one another, even when the system has screwed you, and after a full minute I was grimacing and I hated all three of them, even though under normal circumstances I hated only one, who was very performatively virtuous and often insisted on telling you about the meaningful conversations she had had with janitors or homeless people or about the healthy, nourishing wholewheat bread she'd baked that afternoon.

Bhadveer said, 'I'm trying to determine whether observing group hugs makes me more or less uncomfortable than participating in them.'

'If you were participating, at least you could cop a feel,' I said.

'I like the way you think, Flaherty.' Bhadveer always called me by my last name. Then he said, 'Are Genevieve and Tom in an open marriage?' Genevieve was a second-year poet, and Tom was her husband, who worked a normal-person job, possibly in IT.

'Not that I know of,' I said. 'Why?'

'Because she's totally macking on Milo tonight. Look.' Now that Bhadveer pointed it out, I saw that, across the room, Genevieve and a first-year named Milo were sitting extremely close together on a couch, talking intensely.

I said, 'Is her husband here?'

'By all indications, no.'

I scanned the room, and beyond it the front door, which every minute or two opened to admit more people.

'Doug isn't here, either, if that's who you're really looking for,' Bhadveer said.

'Have you heard that everyone thinks the fourth Peaslee is Aisha?'

Bhadveer made a scoffing noise.

'Why not?' I said.

'Other than because her work sucks?'

I was genuinely surprised. 'Aisha's work doesn't suck. Anyway, Larry's work sucks, and they gave him a Peaslee.'

'I'm not saying she's dumb,' Bhadveer said. 'She got through medical school. She's just not a good writer.'

I furrowed my brow. 'Is the subtext of this conversation racial?'

'It wasn't, but it can be if you want. Enlighten me, oh suburban white girl.' He took a sip of beer and added, 'Aisha is gorgeous, right?'

I nodded.

'Great literature has never been produced by a beautiful woman.'

I stared at him for a few seconds. 'That's ridiculous.'

'Name a book. I'll wait.'

'Virginia Woolf was a babe.' Of the many foolish things I said in graduate school, this is the one that haunts me the most. But I didn't regret it immediately.

Bhadveer shook his head. 'You're thinking of that one picture taken when she was, like, nineteen. And it's kind of sideways, right? To obscure her long face. Why the long face, Virginia?'

I named a writer who had finished our program two years before we arrived, who was rumored to have received a half-million-dollar advance for her first novel. 'Have you seen her in real life?' Bhadveer asked, and I admitted I hadn't. He said, 'She does the best with what she has, but she's not beautiful.' Then he added, 'Don't take this the wrong way, but there tends to be an inverse relationship between how hot a woman is and how good a writer. Exhibit A is George Eliot.'

'That's literally the dumbest idea I've ever heard,' I said.

'It's because you need to be hungry to be a great writer, and beautiful women aren't hungry. Go ahead and contradict me.'

'Joan Didion,' I said. 'Alice Munro. Louise Erdrich.' But providing counterexamples felt distasteful rather than satisfying. I stood. 'I could pretend that I'm going to refill my cup, but really I just want to get away from you.'

As I walked out of the living room, the group hug finally broke apart.

The man with the cult following had arrived and was surrounded by a crowd in the dining room. I stood near a platter of program-sponsored cheese. I could get no closer to him than eight feet, not that I would have tried to speak to him directly, anyway.

'It's tin lunch pails at Yaddo,' he was saying. 'The picnic baskets are at MacDowell.'

Someone nudged me. 'I heard he likes getting blown by young women,' Bhadveer murmured. 'Maybe you should volunteer.'

'Why would I do that?' I murmured back.

'Because then he'll help you get published.'

'First of all,' I said, still murmuring, 'I would never give a blow job to a man in his forties. Well, not until *I'm* in my forties. Or at least my late thirties. Second of all, you seem really obsessed with blow jobs tonight.'

'Flaherty, I'm always obsessed with blow jobs.'

I rolled my eyes. 'You should thank me for setting you up for that.'

Bhadveer tapped his beer bottle against my plastic cup of water. 'Thank you.'

Was I imagining it, or had the question just arisen of whether I'd ever give a blow job to Bhadveer? Was he semi-ineptly flirting or simply sharing his sincere thoughts?

I said, 'Are you already hammered?'

'Yes,' he said, but it was hard to know which narrative this information supported.

We were quiet, and I began listening again to the man with the cult following, who was describing a recent dog-sled trip in Alaska he'd written about for a men's magazine.

'Wait,' I murmured to Bhadveer. 'Clarice Lispector.'

Bhadveer looked momentarily confused then shook his head. He said, 'Clarice Lispector was nothing special.'

'Doug isn't coming tonight,' Dorothy said. 'I just heard from Harold that he's afraid you got a Peaslee, and he doesn't want you rubbing it in his face.'

'Wow,' I said. 'How flattering and insulting.'

'I was on my way to tell you it's okay for you to drink after all when I suddenly realized how to fix my story. I should shift it all to the omniscient point of view. Don't you think? Then I can include the innkeeper's backstory, and people won't be distracted wondering how the servants know all those details about him.' Dorothy had been working on the same story since August. It was set in Virginia in 1810, it fluctuated between twenty and twenty-six pages long, and every sentence in it was exquisite. As a whole, however, it lacked momentum. Several times, she had revised it significantly, and it always turned out equally exquisite and equally lacking in momentum.

'Sure,' I said. 'I don't see why not.'

'I'm going to go try.'

'Now?'

Dorothy nodded.

In another life – if I were still in college – I would have protested. But here it was understood that work, in whatever fashion and on whatever schedule you managed to produce it, took precedence over everything else. This is the lesson of graduate school I am most grateful for. 'Want to get break-fast tomorrow?' I said. 'You can tell me how it went.'

'Definitely,' Dorothy said. 'But call me tonight when you get your mail. No matter what time it is, call me.'

'Bhadveer said he thinks Aisha is too beautiful to be a good writer,' I said. 'He was just expounding on how great literature has never been written by a beautiful woman.'

Dorothy made a face. 'Aisha's not beautiful,' she said.

There was a line outside the first-floor bathroom, so I went upstairs and opened the door to one of the bedrooms that I knew had a bathroom. A standing light in the bedroom was on, and atop the mattress Genevieve and Milo – the married second-year poet and the first-year who wasn't her husband – were lying with their limbs entangled, making out. If I'd been drinking, I probably would have apologized and backed away. But being sober when everyone else seemed increasingly drunk was like wearing a cape that made me invisible. Surely it didn't matter if I quickly peed adjacent to Genevieve and Milo's foreplay?

Indeed, they barely looked up, and insofar as they did I'm not sure they recognized me. Genevieve and her husband soon got divorced, and eventually she and Milo married, and later they became born-again, and now they have six – six! – children. Although I haven't seen either of them for years, I have the sense that I was present at the Big Bang of their family, except for the fact that I'm guessing their family doesn't believe in the Big Bang.

At the bottom of the staircase, I saw Bhadveer again. 'Arundhati Roy?' I said. I no longer had any idea if I was joking.

His expression was dismissive. 'Don't pander.'

Around midnight, the party started dwindling. Some people were dancing to 'Brick House' in the living room and a participant in the group hug was crying in the kitchen, but a steady stream of guests were leaving. The knowledge that I wouldn't be hungover the next morning was so pleasing that at intervals I actively savored it, like a twenty-dollar bill I'd found in my pocket. Really, why did I ever drink?

I was talking to Cecilia, she of the space bubble, when one of the people who lived in the house, a woman named Jess, approached me and said, 'Is it true you're sober?'

When I confirmed that I was, she asked if I'd drive the man with the cult following to his hotel. She said, 'You can take my car, and I'll pick it up tomorrow.'

In the living room, she introduced me to him. She said, 'Ruthie will be your chauffeur.'

He bowed clumsily.

Jess's car turned out to be a pale-blue Honda sedan with a plastic hula-girl figurine hanging from the rear-view mirror. I wondered, of course, if the man would try to elicit a blow job. But from our first seconds alone together I could tell he wasn't going to, and I was both relieved and faintly, faintly insulted. Other than the fact that I was driving, the situation reminded me of when I was in high school and got rides home from dads after babysitting.

'Are you a first- or second-year?' the man asked as I turned onto the street that ran along the park.

'First,' I said.

The man chuckled a little. 'Dare I ask if you're a Peaslee?'

Because I didn't want to bore a successful writer with the details of my unreceived mail, I said, 'I'm not. Peaslees didn't exist when you were in the program, did they?'

'No, they did,' he said. 'It was only fourteen years ago that I graduated from here. And I was a Peaslee. Not to boast.' The man had written six books, more than one of which had been nominated for a major prize. His work had been translated into many languages, and he was a tenured professor at a prestigious school in California. As we crossed the river, he chuckled again and said, 'Fourteen years probably sounds like a long time to you, doesn't it? Someday, it won't.'

The car was silent – I did and didn't believe him – and he said, 'Do you like the program?'

'I love it,' I said. 'I mean, some people are annoying. But even the annoying ones – they're usually annoying in interesting ways.'

'Are you familiar with the narcissism of small differences?'

'I can probably infer what it is, but no.'

'Freud stole the concept from an English anthropologist named Ernest Crawley. It explains the infighting among groups whose members have far more in common than not. I've always thought that if any two students in the program were co-workers at a big company, they'd become close friends. They'd be thrilled to find another person who cares about what they care about, who thinks about things instead of just sleepwalking. But when you're in the program there's such an abundance of kindred spirits to choose from that those same two people might be mortal enemies.'

I thought of the performatively virtuous woman from the group hug and then of Bhadveer. After tonight, was Bhadveer on my shit list or were we about to start dating?

'Are you a good writer?' the man asked.

I laughed. 'That's a totally subjective question.'

'Do you think you're a good writer? Would you enjoy your work if someone else had written it?'

'Yes,' I said. 'I would.'

'That's important. Hold onto it. Oh, and don't marry anyone from the program. If you do, you'll both end up cheating. Hell, if you're a writer, you'll probably cheat on whoever you marry. But you might as well decrease your odds.'

Being the driver was making me feel like a kind of program ambassador, and it was in this capacity, as I stopped at the last light before the hotel, that I said, 'Is there anything you need that you don't have?' I meant a toothbrush, but as soon as I said it I wondered if I'd offered him a blow job.

He seemed sad, though, and not lecherous, when he said, 'Sweetheart, there aren't enough hours in the day to tell you all the things I need and don't have.'

Since I didn't own a car, it felt strange to park in front of my own apartment; it was distracting enough that there were maybe three seconds when I wasn't thinking about my funding letter. But by the time I unlocked my mailbox, which hung on an exterior wall of the house, my hands were shaking.

The envelope was by itself, the only mail I'd received. It was white, with the address of the program embossed in black in the upper left corner. 'Dear Ruth,' the letter started. 'For the 1998–99 academic year, we are pleased to offer you a Ryland W. Peaslee Fellowship in the amount of $8,800.'

I screamed, and then I realized what I'd done, which

was to scream at one in the morning. Also – really – I thought that now I'd probably never give Bhadveer a blow job. Giving a blow job to a Peaslee, it turned out, wasn't the best I could do, the closest I could get.

In the almost twenty years that have passed since that night, I have written – have had published – seven novels; all except the first two were best-sellers. As it happens, my novels are considered 'women's fiction'. This is an actual term used by both publishers and bookstores, and means something only slightly different from 'gives off the vibe of ten-year-old girls at a slumber party.' Several times a year, I travel to speak to auditoriums of five hundred people, no more than a handful of whom are men. On occasion, none are men.

While I'm sure I've sold more books, it's Bhadveer who has attained the status we all believed ourselves to be aspiring to back then – his novels are prominently reviewed, he wins prizes (not yet the Pulitzer, though no doubt it's only a matter of time), he's regularly interviewed on public radio about literary culture. He's the kind of writer, I trust, about whom current students in the program have heated opinions; I'm the kind of writer their mothers read while recovering from knee surgery. To be clear, I'm mocking neither my readers nor myself here – it took a long time, but eventually I stopped seeing women as inherently ridiculous.

A few years ago, by coincidence, Bhadveer and I both gave readings on the same night in Portland, Oregon. His was at an independent bookstore, and mine was at a library, and we were staying at the same hotel. We hadn't kept in touch, but I'd asked my publicist to reach out to his publicist to see if he'd like to get a drink, which we did in the hotel bar. Bhadveer had grown into a handsome man – he was no longer skinny but seemed very fit and also trendily dressed – and I found his company almost intolerable. He name-dropped the magazine editors who courted him and the famous people who were fans of his work and the festivals he'd attended in China and Australia. (I didn't say that I, too, had been invited to all the international festivals, though I hadn't gone, because my children were still young then.) He went out of his way to convey that he hadn't read my books, which is never necessary; writers can tell by a lack of specificity. I felt sad at how much I disliked him. I also felt sad that he called me not Flaherty, not even Ruthie, but just Ruth.

At the end of an hour, during which he consumed three Old-Fashioneds and I had one glass of red wine, he said, 'It's funny that no one other than us is at all successful, isn't it? Besides Grant, obviously.'

Both Bhadveer's career and mine are overshadowed by that of someone who was a virtual nonentity in graduate school, a very quiet guy who went on to write screenplays for which he's twice won an Oscar. He then started directing movies as well, movies that are violent, stylized and enormously popular; if there are any women in them, they're usually raped and often decapitated. This is all bewildering to me, because in graduate school I was under the impression that Grant admired my writing, my slumber-party fiction, more than any of my other male classmates did. Though we almost never spoke, his typed critiques were unequivocally complimentary and encouraging. It's for this reason that, despite his misogyny-flavored mega-success, I wish him well.

In the hotel bar, I said to Bhadveer, 'Well, Harold has that collection, right? And Marcy has two novels.'

'That have sold, what, twelve copies combined? I gave Harold a blurb out of pity, but I couldn't get through the first story.'

I tried to decide whether to be nice or honest, then said, 'Yeah, neither could I.'

'Think about it,' Bhadveer said. 'Jeff's not a writer. Dorothy's not a writer. Your boy Doug's not a writer. Aisha's not a writer.'

'You know the experiment in the seventies with the blue-eyed and brown-eyed students?' I said. 'I sometimes wonder if we're like that.'

'But Jonah and Larry were Peaslees with us, and neither of them is a writer.'

As I said, this was a while back. It took months to determine how I wished I'd replied, which is: Yes, you can say whether people have published books. But you don't get to say whether they're writers. Some of them are probably working on books now that they'll eventually finish and sell; some of them probably haven't written fiction for years and might never again. But the way they inhabit the world, the way they observe it – of course they're writers.

———

On that long-ago night when I opened the letter at one in the morning, perhaps thirty seconds passed between my scream and Lorraine's door opening. She hurried out in a white silk slip and matching bathrobe and said with alarm, 'Ruthie, are you okay?'

I extended the letter toward her. 'I got a Peaslee! I'm a Peaslee!'

Lorraine hesitated, and I was startled. Was it possible that even inside our university, across the small divide of two similar programs, the significance of the Peaslee didn't translate?

'The fellowship!' I added. 'I got the best kind of fellowship for next year!'

'Oh, Ruthie, how wonderful,' she said, and she stepped forward and hugged me tightly.

An Exclusive Q&A
with Curtis Sittenfeld

What is it about short stories that draws you to the form? Can you talk about what you really relished while writing these stories?

I love how short stories can be intense all the way through. Most novels, including mine, have some slackness, but a short story can remain tight and propulsive. Frankly, I also find them easier and more manageable to write, much less messy than writing novels. Without question, there are rewards to writing novels, but after a year or two or three, I almost always end up sick of my own novel. I think it's harder for the reader or the writer to get sick of a story.

Your stories confront our own weaknesses and yet feel fully compassionate towards the characters. Are you aware of achieving this balance or does it emerge organically?

I'd say it emerges organically. I certainly believe that we're all flawed, so a person being flawed doesn't mean they're unworthy of compassion. I also feel that either a character being honest about herself or a writer being honest about a character – freely acknowledging that the character has some unappealing qualities instead of pretending she's only endearing – often makes me like the character more. I don't look to fictional characters to be moral role models – perhaps the opposite.

Can you name your favourite short story? And what did you learn from it about technique and also about human nature?

My all-time favourite writer, for almost thirty years, has been Alice Munro. If I had to pick a favourite story, it would be very hard, but perhaps 'The Albanian Virgin'? Or 'Tricks'? Or 'The Love of a Good Woman'?

I admire everything she does – how she immerses the reader deep in the protagonist's situation; how she's fearless about showing casual bad behaviour; how her plots are complicated and jump across decades; how sharp her insights are; and, above all, how she captures the authentic texture of life.

Finally, do you feel surprised by the turn your stories take, or do you have them already mapped in your mind before you start to write? Are any of them ever even slightly autobiographical?

I sometimes borrow a bit from real life – a line a friend said, or an actual article of clothing I saw, or a meal I ate – but I wouldn't say the stories are autobiographical in the sense that the protagonists are not stand-ins for me. I often know that I'm ready to write a short story when I have two ideas that intersect in a way where I suspect they'll enrich each other. For instance, 'White Women LOL' has the racist-viral-video plotline *and* the lost-dog plotline, and 'Show Don't Tell' has the fellowship competition *and* the neighbour. All that said, I definitely surprise myself in the act of writing, and that's a huge part of the fun.

Curtis Sittenfeld is the *Sunday Times* and *New York Times* bestselling author of *Rodham* and *American Wife*. Other acclaimed bestselling novels include *Prep*, *The Man of My Dreams*, *Sisterland* (a Richard and Judy bookclub pick) and *Eligible*. She is also the author of an acclaimed short-story collection *You Think It, I'll Say It*, and has been shortlisted for the *Sunday Times* EFG Short Story Award. Her stories have appeared in the *New Yorker*, *Esquire*, *Oprah* magazine, the *New York Times* magazine and elsewhere. *Help Yourself* is her latest collection of stories to be published in the UK. Sittenfeld is also the guest editor for the 2020 *Best American Short Stories* anthology. She lives with her family in Minneapolis, Minnesota. Follow her on Twitter @CSittenfeld.